Now Jesus
by Omar Corazo

Dedicated to the Chrysalis Alternative School. You were killed in your prime by the every day evils of sell outs, corrupt lying administrators and public apathy, but not before you saved many lives, mine being one of them.

Contents

Now Jesus

Shit, fool, you know that chick Lydia Mares, fool, the one whose mom won like, shit, I don't even know, like a million dollars at the casino? She gots that custom pink Escalade, fool.

Yeah, that's a bitchass color, fool, but that shit's tight, fool. She got Miguel to put 32 inch spinner rims on it, fool. I saw Lydia and Eduardo and all them North Side pussies cruising it out at Suazo's party on Friday.

Yeah, I saw them out there, rolling it, fool. I rode in it one time. That ride's sick as hell, fool—cherry stereo, sub-woofers, leather seats. She had TV screens and PS2 players installed in the back seats, fool. But I wouldn't never paint no Caddie pink, fool. That's fucked up. Shit.

I know, fool. A ride like that has to be black, fool.

Or blue, fool. Southside blue.

I hear that!

Anyway, I guess that Lydia told Martin's chick— that little Amanda chick from the Middle School—that she likes me, fool, and that we were, like, fucking around or some shit, like that I kissed her that time when we were all drunk on Crown and Redbull and cocopuffing and popping all kinds of hydros with Lisa Valerio and Pricilla Cortez and all them hos at The Dips, and now Lil' Pit's all fucking crazy pissed, fool. He told Sylvester he's gonna fuck me up bad when he sees me. It's bullshit, fool. I never really even talked to that dumb bitch since 7th Grade and I only even talked to her then cuz I was boning her friend Angela. It's all fucked up. Lil' Pit's crazy, fool.

The shorter of the two boys—both in their late teens, swarthy and lean with gelled back black hair— sucked at his cigarette and shook his head appreciatively. Obviously Lil' Pit was no one to cross. He shook his head again and made a short whistling sound.

That's fucked up, fool. I saw Lil' Pit beat the shit out of Droopy with a wrench that one time over at Adam Trujillo's trailer, fool.

I heard about that, but fuck it, fool. I already told my cousin Penky what happened and he said he'll call in the Juaritos if Lil' Pit wants to bang, fool. Those fuckers are bad, fool—the Juaritos—you don't wanna mess with them, ese.

Penky met one in the pinta last year, fool, that dude Ruiz, fool. He was the one who was up here for the fiestas with a Rottweiler on, like, a big chain, fool. He had his 9 right on his belt the whole time, fool, walking around the whole time just like that and the cops didn't tell him nothing.

Luis Markel, the teacher on duty 20 feet away, leaned against the north wall of the school building looking at a Quonset hut across a fallow, rutted, dusty field fenced in with razor wire. He stared lazily into the middle distance—his grey flecked eyes moving between the Quonset hut and a small faded Gospel of Christ Church sign mounted on two creosote posts at its entrance—but he listened intently to the boys' talk. At intervals he looked at his shoes to mask his eaves-dropping—doing so gave the appearance of a reverie: something for which he was famous among his students. He let an instinctive ten seconds pass and again stared squinting at the sign and church. A solitary crow rooted through a clump of asters growing out of a small mound in the far corner of the field—the only things living on what must have been three acres of agriculturally zoned land. During breaks in the staff room, Al, the old head teacher whose stubborn pastoral worldview had been formed during thirty years of service in this remote building, had spoken ruefully for months of the inevitable expansion of what he called the Gospel of Christ *complex*. He'd sat in on county planning meetings: the trashy Quonset hut and interminable rows of sheds would be replaced with a modern set of glass buildings and outbuildings. The field would be surfaced and used to park worshippers' cars. *The Lord will always need new parking lots,* Markel thought. Mark it down to the progress of man.

The boys were speaking again.

You seen them photos of Britney Spear's pussy, fool?

Nah, dude, ha, ha, ha. Shit. Is she hot, or what?

Not even, fool! Her shit looks like an overcooked roast beef with a little hair glued on it.

Ha, ha, ha. You're fucking sick, fool.

Markel looked at his shoes again so that his face couldn't be seen. He smiled slightly, invisibly. You had to choose your wars with these students. At times their raw, pitiful, profane minds were hilarious. The two boys, still snickering, not pausing from their cigarettes, looked simultaneously down the gravel road to the highway. A familiar middle-aged woman in a Lincoln Town car with a Christian fish symbol embossed on the front grill drove past the school building and outer smoking area toward the Gospel of Christ Church looking straight in front of her. She sat stiffly, head unmoving. Her face, bony and severe, heavily made up, dissolved into a freakishly long, wrinkled throat that warbled as she drove over the washboards in the road. Her huge blue poodle—Markel had heard somewhere that it was a fifth generation clone—panted and perked in the back seat. Even though she never looked at the school grounds when passing, every one of the staff and students somehow knew her frigid, oyster-eyed, disapproving stare. One of the Gospel of Christ's premier parishioners. The taller, nervous, talkative boy yelled, *Hallelujah*, at the car, then muttered, *giraffe honky bitch*, when it passed. His friend laughed. Both smoked with a special intensity: the bell would ring soon.

Three girls walked out of the kitchen exit and turned toward several broken desks strewn under a Chinese Elm near the back gate. The two boys were silent watching them approach. In the sudden quiet, Markel could just hear a ring of other boys beat boxing, busting flows, ciphering at the far end of the smoking area. *This niggaz demonic, atomic, I smokes the chronic....* Starlings flocked and chittered in the denuded vertical branches of a row of poplars lining the dry ditch at the school property boundary. Half a mile away through a hedge of wild plum and black locust trees, Markel could see multicolored blurs and streaks of cars on the highway. Part of a billboard advertising no-snip, thirty minute, anesthesia free vasectomies was visible. He shifted against the wall to watch the girls pass. The nearest smiled and said, *Hey Mister*. He nodded at all three, still smiling faintly. Each girl had long, meticulously tended, jet black Aztec hair, thick glossed lips and giant stylized black indigenous eyes that they made look even larger with excesses of liner and mascara. Each wore hiphugging jeans and a black, lowcut T-shirt with the Playboy Bunny logo outlined in flashing metallic sequins across the bosom. Each carried matching Tinkerbell purses and had the word *RISKY* tattooed in dull green ink along what they called their *fuck you finger*.

As they passed, the taller boy wet his thumb on

his tongue and used it to extinguish his cigarette butt. He dropped the butt at his feet, cocked his head, drew his blank, dark, simian features into a sneer and said, *Close your fucking legs, Esther. It smells like chunky tuna out here,* to the girl who had greeted Markel. All three girls' faces curdled with identical hatred. *Fuck you, you little puto!* Esther shouted back. Markel sprung from the wall and took a step toward the boy as the bell rang. He beckoned. The boy, who had been smirking at the three snarling girls while his friend laughed, grimaced, rolled his eyes and head and tisked at Markel.

Shit! Whatchoo want, fool?

Markel looked at him tiredly. *Come with me, Jesus.*

Why, fool? I didn't do shit. I was just messing around.

You need to think about what comes out of your mouth.

The boy grinned and waited a canny nanosecond for the right beat.

And you need to think about what goes into *your mouth, fool. Like my big, brown, hairy nutsack.*

The shorter boy turned his back to Markel and laughed in a high, squeaky, hysterical pitch.

Come with me NOW, *Jesus,* Markel said, knowing the boy would be suspended for a day, would revel in being thought a hard case by his peers, would return on Monday with his mother, Esperanza, a twenty-nine-year-old woman who looked as though she had come out of the birth canal florid, blowsy, blasted and smoking an LPC. Before the conference in the therapy room—a converted supplies closet—Janie Starks, the school counselor, would remind Markel in a low conspiratorial voice that the only time Jesus Junior had ever had any contact with his father was when a drunken Jesus Senior had taken his five-year-old son to the Gorge with a cardboard box full of mongrel puppies that he doused one by one in gasoline, set afire and threw off the bridge.

I mean, I'm not excusing his behavior, Janie was guaranteed to say. *Everyone has to be responsible for their own choices, but we have to remember where these kids come from. You know? I mean, this is just the population we're serving. We have to advocate for these kids because no one else is going to do it. I mean, my God, look at Esperanza. She was arrested twice last year for soliciting men in bars and luring them into back alleys to be mugged. Do you think she has the resources to help Jesus?*

. . .

During his prep period, Markel sat in a tatty plush chair in the office examining a frieze of sleighs, bells and reindeer that Darla, the receptionist had cut out of silver paper and hung across the entryway as Christmas decoration five months earlier. Someone had finally taken it down and laid it in a tangle by an empty open box of cake donuts on the only table in the room. Mrs. Newcomb and Mrs. Gomez, the two teaching aides, sat on a couch in the corner behind the Coke machine talking about their plans for the mini-break. Mrs. Newcomb's plaid skirt was hiked up high enough that Markel could see—beneath her bargain stockings—the varicose veins on her shins. Mrs. Gomez sipped from an extra-large cup of McDonald's coffee and left lipstick marks on its rim.

I hope Teddy takes me out on Saturday because his mother's visiting Sunday and Monday and we've just been going, going, going, gosh, since December. Mrs. Gomez shook her head at the recollection of her hectic schedule.

Mrs. Newcomb smoothed her skirt and sighed wryly.

We can't even think about going out since Daniel's colonoscopy. The doctors found I don't know how many polyps. Thank God they aren't any of them cancerous, but they bleed like crazy. Yesterday Daniel was joking with our granddaughter, Deborah—she's back from community college for two weeks—he was just joking, but he says to her real straight-faced, he says: Deb, I may need to borrow one of your pads, I'm bleeding so bad. *It was funny when he said it, but it's real, real scary when he bleeds like that, my gosh.*

. . .

Markel stood in his customary place for duty on second break listening now to three new boys sharing their most tender insights.

You ever given a girl a jelly donut, fool?

Nah, what's that?

It's when you cum in her face and then punch her in the nose till she bleeds, fool.

. . .

Markel gave a practiced look of dismay at the newspaper article he'd just read aloud to a small group of first stream literacy students.

Alright, so what does everyone think of this? This woman—maybe some of you know her; she lives on the Llano, out on Calle Cielo—she's chosen to have fourteen children. Wow. Fourteen kids. What impact do you think this choice has had on her life?

Eduardo Reyes stopped popping his gum and grinned.

It probably means her snatch is all blown out and shit.

The class laughed. Markel's face clenched; his eyes slit. Druzella, one of the boy's several girlfriends, spoke quickly to intervene.

That's not really a bad thing to say, mister. It's true. Is there any, like…like…um, scientific way you could say it so that it don't sound bad?

Markel was relieved. He was too weary for another confrontation and possible suspension and Druzella's tactic was deft enough to give everyone an out.

Yeah, what's the scientific way to say that? Reyes echoed, reaching compulsively for the enormous bling bling bangle—a sneering zirconium skull—hanging on his skinny neck.

What you want to say—and please believe me, you will all be well served in learning to frame your statements and questions respectfully and thoughtfully—what you want to say is that this woman's reproductive organs and health could be adversely *affected by having this many children. Who knows what the word adversely means?*

…

Three minutes after the final bell, Markel sat at his desk reading a composition written by one of his 9th Graders under the given title, What Success Means to Me.

$ucess is wen you got all kind of money & bitches & be rollin it in a bad car don't nobuddy fuck wit u cuz u a fucking G fool….

Carl, the Math teacher walked into the room—
sauntered in.

Have you seen your girlfriend today?

Which one?

Starks.

Yes, I've seen her. Why?

Did you see her new haircut?

It's more a hairstyle.

*You should have told her she needs to lose 100 pounds
if she wants to look like a Charley's Angel.*

You're a scaly bastard.

I heard you had some disciplinary problems at lunch.

*Yeah. Your star pupil was frothing at the mouth. Al
had to call the sheriff's department. They sent some new
deputy—he had a stuffed purple chimpanzee doll hanging
on that wire mesh that separated the back and front seats of
his cruiser.*

That's funny. Cute. Who got in trouble? Reyes?

*No, it was your little pet, Jesus. Shit, Reyes is a saint
nowadays. Now that Starks put him back on his meds. He
told me last week he was going to live the rest of his life
with his mother out in that trailer court on the Llano selling weed, raising Rotties, collecting disability and playing
Scarface Takes Over Miami on his Xbox all day every day.*

Ha. At least he has a plan. What are Rotties?

Rottweilers, buddy. You've got to keep up with the lingo.

So Reyes wants to use my hard earned tax dollars to fund his early retirement?

It's probably better than paying to have him locked up in a jail cell—which is the only alternative.

That's a bunch of cack. You want to put private prison investors out of business? This country would collapse. The only alternative is for all of the weeping heart liberals who set school disciplinary policy to piss off into the void and let us put shock collars on these little beasts. Reyes was destined for a jail cell from the minute the doctor slapped his wrinkly little ass. The only thing that might save him when he is finally put in a cage is that Virgin Mary tattoo on his back. As for Jesus, they should just give him a gun and all the crack cocaine he wants and drop him on the front line in Iran.

It's good to hear you haven't lost any of your youthful idealism working here.

We should be training these kids to be snipers and putting them up on the roof of Wal-Mart to clean house and keep the population stable. They'd be doing a civic duty.

You should teach Social Studies. Yeesh. Anyway, what kind of lunatic shit are you getting up to tonight?

We'll probably go out with Leonard and some of his friends. Last Friday he bet me $200 I wouldn't swallow a live Chinese Beta Fish out of his aquarium. I downed it with a shot of Jager. Easiest money I ever made.

You're a pillar of this community.

. . .

Twenty minutes after the final bell, Markel stood in an automated Alphix checkout line holding a pint of vodka and a lemon. Two thickset, ruddy, coarse men in dirty coveralls stood behind him speaking in broad, twanging country accents. These were the new home-spun class of men who had come to town to work the second home building boom, (as the Chamber of Commerce called it). Markel liked them better than the carpetbaggers who sat in the El Mundo bar sipping $150 glasses of Louis XVII cognac, discussing how to sell the county off plat by plat. A little girl in pigtails wearing her pajamas decorated with clowns and umbrellas, licking the wrapper of a Butterfinger, walked up to one of the men and pulled at his pocket.

Daddy, I cain't find the ticket you said for Grand-maw.

Markel saw the hand the man placed on the girl's tiny head. It looked like a rootball: outsized, gnarled, scabbed at the knuckles, covered in engine oil.

Go back air 'n tell the man you want a Diamond Dazzler. Your Gran said she felt lucky tonight for a Diamond Dazzler.

The girl moved off looking uncertainly back at

her father. The men resumed speaking.

What's this I hear you're goin' to Florida for a week juss when we gittin' the drywall punched in?

My old man passed. He was livin' in a retirement home out there near Orlando. He had a almost new Chrysler he left me—I think it's an '09—but he juss parked it under one a them papaya trees in the yard there and never drove it, so it's got good miles but it's covered in grackle shit about that thick.

The man speaking—formed strangely with extremely long legs and a stumpy torso—held up his rough thumb and index finger in a pinch to show the thickness of accumulated grackle shit.

Shit or no, I wish I had me a new Chrysler, man.

Yeah, well, if wishes was fishes we'd all be up to our assholes in carp, son.

Both men guffawed.

Speakin' of shit and what's good....

The girl returned stomping and sighing and held out a lottery ticket for her father to inspect.

This oooooone, Daddy? Her voice was exaggeratedly peevish.

Naw, Mabel, I told you, Diamond Dazzler. Your Gran won't take nuthin' else. Go back there and ask the man to help you.

There ain't nobody back there. He left.

Well go over to the counter and wait there so if you get the ticket we can get outta here when I'm done.

The girl sagged, exasperated. *Where do they learn all those dramatic tricks so soon?* Markel thought.

What-ever, the girl said frowning. She stomped off again and her father looked at his friend, chuckling.

Kids, man. She's in a big hurry cause I'm takin' 'em all down to Long John Silvers tonight for the popcorn shrimp special. Anyway, I was sayin', man, you seen that new secretary over in the transport pool? The little dark one? Christ alive man, I'd eat me a mile a salty peanuts straight outta her shit juss to lick where it come from, boy.

Haw! Yeah, man. She look like she can grind and chuck it, alright.

. . .

In the narrow street where he had parked behind the Alphix, Markel could see a plump woman in a terrycloth bathrobe and curlers smoking a cigarette and scowling at him through the window of a prefab house on the saltbush plain at the edge of town. Beyond a file of more prefab houses there was a cyclone fence around three propane tanks and then miles of flat gullied malpais that ended in conical hills backlit by the marl colored sky. It would be dark in ten minutes. It was already cold. Markel yelled *Fuck!* again at the sidewalk. The hood of his car was opened and he peered at the engine uncomprehendingly. He shook his head and whispered, *fuck.*

Oh my God! Hey mister! Long time! What's up?

Markel turned—still uncomprehending—to the girl who had come up the sidewalk behind him.

Are you stuck, or what, Mister? The girl asked cheerfully.

Yes, Markel answered. *I think it's the, uh, alternator, but I'm not sure.*

He shrugged at the girl. She wore a faux-fur, blue-shot, leopardprint overcoat and matching knee-high boots with four-inch stiletto heels. Her hair was cut very short and dyed powder blue. Her lip and septum were pierced. She sensed Markel had no idea of what he was seeing.

It's me, Mister Markel. Rachel.

Markel's eyes rounded even more. *Oh, wow! Of course! I didn't recognize you. You've changed a lot in, what is it, three years? I mean, you were always a dresser, but....* He gestured with both of his hands at her. The girl gave her long body and jungle couture a practiced glance and said, *I know. Everyone says that. Do you need a ride somewheres?*

Markel smiled widely. *I do. I do. I would appreciate it, Rachel.* He looked at her shopping cart. *Can I help you with that?* He looked at the cart's contents: a bottle of Courvoisier, two bags of spicy hot pork rinds and a carton of Pall-Malls were placed haphazardly on top of a mound of Twinkies boxes.

I guess you haven't remembered all those nutritional health tips, Ms. Starks used to give you. They were good tips, even if she never exactly followed them herself.

Oh, ha, ha, yeah, well, I eat pretty good and stuff. Like, I go to Subway all the time. I'm just really busy. The Twinkies are for my little girl for dessert and stuff.

I'd heard you'd had a baby. Congratulations. That must be an adventure.

Oh yeah! Yeah, it is! I love my little girl!

The girl took a set of keys from her Chloe hand-bag and deactivated the alarm of a light blue Humvee parked two cars up from Markel's stalled Cougar.

. . .

As they turned onto the highway, Markel was silent for a moment remembering Rachel's father. He had raised two daughters alone in a ramshackle trailer off the interstate by traveling across the country selling bowling trophies to mom and pop alleys in a million small towns. Elton Lubin—that was his name—but he was always called Grubbs for some unknown reason. Markel had only ever seen him dressed in check shirts and slacks with suspenders. He had taken Markel aside during a parent conference to give a piece of blunt advice after Markel's all too public divorce:

Listen kid, I'm just an old shitbird, been living in this place with these spicks since I was 9 years old. I smoke three packs of Luckies a day, I barely make a buck hustling my ass raw all over America, my wife was a big blown up balloon of a bitch who left me as soon as she could—I only got one thing to say to you: Go out and get yourself some pussy, boy, get yourself some red snapper and you'll forget all the rest real quicklike.

Markel had last seen him two years ago slumped in a wheelchair parked in front of a table at the Burger King outdoor section. Elton could barely move his arm and had an oxygen tube in his nose, but sat smoking a Camel while a raven stood eating his hamburger inches away. *What's going on, Elton? You're losing your lunch,* Markel said. The bird flew off, croaking evilly. *My goddamned vertebrae are fused together,* Elton snapped. When Markel confronted his caregiver from the municipal retirement home, the squat, pockmarked man in a faded yellowing uniform looked at him balefully and said, *They don't pay me enough to talk to you, asshole.*

The girl turned sharply and accelerated as they passed the Stallion Gas Station on the south side of town. A cluster of lights had come on in the near-dark out on the Llano.

I heard about your father, Markel said. *My condolences.*

Oh, yeah. Yeah. Thanks. He was a tough old guy. It

was alright. After all those years of cancer and dementia and stuff, he just fell asleep. The girl giggled nervously.

Do you still live out this way?

I do, yeah. I still live in the same place. My sister Sarah moved to Los Angeles with her husband last year, so it's just me and my boyfriend and daughter living out at the trailer. Actually, I was hoping you wouldn't mind if we stopped there for a minute. I have to pick something up real quick. Then I could drop you off.

Sure. Of course. That'll be fine. I appreciate you going out of your way. How is Sarah?

She's pretty good. She's got three kids now, three boys. But I guess she went to work as like a sales associate on the phone so that she can stay at home with them and stuff. Her husband drives a truck out there where they live in Utah.

That's good—sounds good. Any work is good work these days.

Yeah. Ha, ha, ha.

Speaking of which, Rachel, if you don't mind my asking, did you rob a bank or hit the Lotto or something? He gestured at the interior of the Humvee. *It looks like you've made some sound investments.*

Ha, ha. You're still so funny, Mister Markel. No, nothing like that. We're doing pretty good, though. Kyle, that's my boyfriend—he's not Britanny, my daughter's father, but he really loves her—anyway, he gets section 8 money every month. That's like disability. It was really hard *to get, you know? Like, he was in a really bad car accident and he still had to keep going back to social services with, like, X-rays and stuff that showed his brain hemorrhages. So he doesn't work too much anymore and we have to keep it real quiet when he does, because we don't want to lose that money, you know? Sometimes he'll go and do those drug trials things, where you take new drugs—like legal drugs for the doctors—for like a week and they give you $5,000—he can go do those because they don't really do a, like a deep background check, you know? Like, they just do a physical and don't really ask too many questions. But that only happens once in a while and he has to go out to L.A. for that. I tried it one time but I didn't like it cuz' they give you so many shots. They also take your eggs for, like, fertility clinics, and stuff. I did that once but, um, they promised me, like, $10, 000, but it was only $2,000 because of the fine print and all that. Then I started working at Cheeky Freaks two nights a week, and I've been there for, um, like a year and a half, so they finally started giving me weekend shifts and I probably make like $3,000 on Friday and Saturday nights.*

Carl had told Markel about Cheeky Freaks, the all-nude strip club that had been built amid short-lived puritanical controversy in the southern industrial wastes of the capital. *$3,000 in two nights*, Markel thought. *That's what I make in a month as a 10 year, level II public school teacher serving youth-at-risk in a school designated as low income by the United States Department of Education.*

Markel said, *I always knew you'd find your way.*

The girl looked at him sideways quickly, giggling.

Thanks, ha, ha, ha. Yeah, it's pretty good money and I like doing it all right.

Markel reflected. She had been gritty, shrewd and adaptive as the only white girl in school. She had worked her way into the largest clique of Hispanic girls and fluently spoke their patois of getting banged into gangs and partying until you puked and passed out. Markel knew that was chameleon acting and that Rachel really would make her way. Now she was out-earning him by standing naked before the world. He'd reserve judgement until he paid his mortgage and fixed his car.

Here we are, Mister. Do you want to come in and meet Kyle and Brittany? I just have to pick something up real quick.

Of course. Rachel, you can call me Luis. You graduated three years ago. You're a young woman now, a mother.

. . .

Markel stood in the small living room of the singlewide trailer looking at Kyle's artwork while Kyle, sprawled on a tatty beige Lazy Boy in shorts and an undershirt, spoke into his cell phone.

Vicodins won't get it, Rico. Uh huh. Right. Yeah. Yeah. Yeah. No, I don't care. That's bullshit. I don't want Vicodins, period. Period, Rico! I want Roxies unless you can get Demerol....

Kyle had to speak loudly because a band that Rachel had identified as Crotch Slime was railing out from two surround sound stereo speakers set on either side of the room. *NC57913! Barcode where her pussy should be!* seemed to be the chorus the lead man was chunking and frothing up out of his throat, but Markel couldn't be sure. In the din, when they'd entered the trailer, Rachel had explained something about Kyle's secondary connections to Crotch Slime. Then, yelling all-out, she'd introduced Markel to her daughter Brittany and disappeared into a back room. Twenty minutes later, Rachel hadn't returned. Brittany sat cooing under a table where the living room became the kitchen. Markel had already watched for five minutes as the little girl dipped her fingers into a plastic container of lime parfait beside her on the linoleum floor, then gleefully thrust them at a high-strung teacup Chihuahua that yipped and licked her whole arm and turned in circles to yowl at a bulldog puppy watching mournfully and pissing on the shag carpet a foot away. Both the Chihuahua and bulldog pup wore rhinestone studded collars.

Kyle was off the phone. He rose from the Lazy Boy, hitching up his shorts. He turned the stereo down and approached Markel.

Sorry I was on the phone, man. Business. What'd you say your name was?

Markel guessed Kyle was maybe thirty-five years old. His face was long, narrow, sharp and pitted with acne scars. His cropped hair was peroxide blond, but his sideburns and sculpted goatee were black. A block silhouette showing a hunched over proto-ape passing through evolutionary stages to become an erect-standing Death Metal guitar player was tattooed on the inside of his left forearm. A two-dimensional iconographic cup of coffee and lit cigarette were tattooed on the inside of his right forearm.

I'm Luis Markel. I used to be Rachel's Language Arts teacher in high school.

Kyle tore open the carton of Pall-Malls Rachel had placed on the small lawn table in front of the Lazy Boy, took out a pack, opened it, took out a cigarette.

No shit, man? That's cool. I'm an artist myself.

So I see.

Kyle lit his cigarette and turned to look at the painting Markel had nodded toward. It was an oil on velvet painting of a grinning Godzilla dressed in a flamboyant cream-colored suit and stiff brim hat with a zebra skin band.

I call that one Pimpzilla, man.

Hunh, interesting. What about that one? Markel pointed to a painting done in the same medium of the cartoon character SpongeBob Square Pants smiling obscenely, wearing a crown of thorns and being crucified.

I don't have a name for that one yet. Hollywood! Kyle turned to the Chihuahua yipping and licking parfait off of Brittany's fingers while the girl shrieked with delight, *Shut the fuck up! Jesus! Sorry about that, man. Those are Rachel's dogs. Come into the bedroom, I've got a whole series in there.*

Rachel was not in the bedroom when they walked in. Kyle spoke through the bathroom door. *Hey baby, I'm in here showing Marcel, sorry, what's your name again, dude? Markel. I'm showing Markel the paintings in here, so don't come out with your titties hanging in the breeze or nothing, ha, ha, ha.* There was a small indiscernible noise from the bathroom. Kyle pointed to a triptych on the wall above a waterbed. *I did that last year. Crotch Slime—that was the band we were just listening to—their front man told a friend of mine they might use these as cover art for the next album.* The paintings—all oil on velvet—were of a woman with a runway model figure lying down, spraddle-legged, giving birth to an AK-47 in the first panel, SpongeBob Square Pants in the second and Pimpzilla in the third. The afterbirth gushing out of her photorealistic genitals was painted vividly: bright crimson splotches spotted with dayglo lime-green dollar signs.

I see how the themes all tie in now. I guess you're going to have to paint Pimpzilla being crucified next.

Oh shit! That's a fucking brilliant idea, man!

Pimpalicious.

Ha, ha! Shit yeah, man! Pimpalicious! I like that!

Markel noticed a bizarre construction on the

night table. He pointed. *What's that?* Kyle switched on a light—a lava lamp. They both stepped nearer to what turned out to be a three-foot-tall tower designed with twisted turrets and several compartments and levels.

I call these ERMs—Executive Roach Motels, man. I make them with toothpicks and glue. I keep cockroaches in the little cells here, see. Kyle pointed through a crosswise line of toothpicks at the shadow of an unmoving cockroach. *When they're full up, I take them out back, burn them and film it. Kind of like performance art, you know?*

I do.

I fucking hate cockroaches, man. Hate 'em. I've got a Mac 10 and 2,000 subsonic rounds of ammo in the closet so that I'm ready for the apocalypse, man. I'll just go around blasting gigantic mutant albino cockroaches in the nuclear ash, man. Bang, bang, bitches! Ha, ha, ha!

It's good to have a plan for all eventualities....

. . .

When she finally emerged from the bedroom, Rachel's eyes were glassed.

I'm so sorry, Mister. I just had to get ready for work. Her tongue was heavy, her words nearly slurred.

Not at all. You're doing me a huge favor. Kyle and I have been talking art and end times.

They drove mainly in silence. The girl hummed numbly through her nose. Markel asked her polite questions that she answered in monosyllables. She had been known at school for being alternately reticent and manically confiding. Apparently she'd already made all of her confessions for the night. She pulled into Markel's apartment block and followed his directions through a circuit of streets and intersections. To the south was cold open desert for over 150 miles. She parked the car in front of number 235. Markel thanked her warmly as he opened his door. She suddenly grabbed his hand.

Um, God, I'm really sorry Mister Markel, that I took so long back there.

No, no, not all. You've helped me so much tonight. You saved me.

Mist…Luis, um. She looked up from the seat between them still holding his hand. She was weeping; her mascara bled and smeared down her cheeks. Snot ran into her mouth. *I, I always…liked you. I liked you so much. Could I, um, God, God, could I come in?*

Markel exhaled slowly. He said, *Oh, Rachel.*

Christ Nothing

It had been such a miserably arctic winter—I'd counted four flickers frozen to the tops of fence posts in January—that I made a point of driving through the greenbelt on the first Saturday of spring break. I pulled onto the side of a single-track dirt road that followed the river valley south through long rectangular fields and neatly planted orchards and sat for several minutes in my car looking at the back of my hands, listening to Prince sing *When You Were Mine*, on KTIZ Radio. When the song ended and the DJ's fizzing voice came on to sell a revolutionary new brand of toothpaste, I got out of the car and walked toward the river under a culvert raised over a sandy wash on bolted square beams.

The first signs of bloom and color were showing in the wasted cadmium yellow rows of mowed alfalfa stalks. An almost imperceptible rose color tinged the rough, scored, black boles of apple and apricot trees. In the nearest field, ground doves walked jerkily around small flocks of sheep to hunt worms from the new black lines of soil a farmer had turned over plowing ditches. Blackbirds hopped along the rusted tines of an old harrow parked under a stripped silk cottonwood. Cows lowed in the next pasture. Two heat-shimmering plateaus converged into a long scarp of desert in the distance. Only the hundreds of empty plastic shooter bottles of Cuervo Gold, Yukon Jack and Jack Daniels thrown into the weed chaff and bull thistle patches by the side of the road gave any indication of a world of manufacturing and liver disease beyond this view. I walked recalling how I'd had to piss into gallon water jugs for four months because my pipes burst in November and I had no money to fix them. I thought of moving back into an apartment, of moving to Florida, of writing a firmly worded letter to my congressman demanding that he double teachers' salaries or get wholly fucked.

An off-the-lot white Chevrolet Suburban stopped beside me as I stepped over bent strands of barbed wire onto a faded trail running across an open, scoured, caliche flat that rounded into stands of tamarisks on the east bank of the river. The passenger's side automatic window hummed down. A handsome big-jawed woman with a frosted coif stuck her head out.

Excuse me. She spoke with a strained, overly controlled diction. Her voice warbled. *I'm sorry. Can you tell us how to get onto I-25?*

I approached the car. It shone and smelled of new vinyl. A toothy waving Arnold Schwarzenegger bobble-head doll was mounted to the dashboard.

I can. You have to turn around and go back along this road about two miles until you come to the intersection—you would've passed it getting here—the three-way intersection right next to a gravel crushing factory....

I know what you mean, the driver said with a vague twang. I bent slightly to address him. He was incredibly small, his face a smooth, slight, bald little oval. He wore what must have been a custom made pastel Ashworth golf shirt tucked into herringbone trousers. A teenage girl sat in the backseat listening to her iPod, swinging her head slightly, chewing gum, staring at me slyly.

I know the intersection you mean. I think that's where we lost it.

I formed my hands into an illustrative V and said, *It's tricky: you have to take the middle road then turn right immediately and follow the feeder road over a mile to get onto the off-ramp for the interstate. I think somebody shot down the sign for the turn off a few months ago and the county hasn't repaired it yet.*

The woman gave me a fast, keen look.

Oh my....

She spoke with a faint scandalized thrill: this was a story she'd tell in her air-conditioned living room in a suburb where the maples were planted in set patterns and the three choices of house design were to code. The man became more attentive too—his close, wet, brown eyes blinked and he turned more fully toward me.

That's something of a surprise. Everyone is always so nice to us when we come here on vacation.

It's mainly a friendly town, but there are still some pretty wild types up in the hills here, I said blandly.

Really? We've been coming out for our vacations ten years and we've never had any problems. The man apparently thought the conversation had become intimate enough to warrant introductions.

I'm Bob Savage, this is my wife Gilda and my daughter Eileen.

I smiled perfunctorily and said, *I'm Luis Markel.*

The man turned and gazed out the windshield of his car; his wife did the same as if cued. *We're really thinking about buying a second place now that I'm retired and you all have built a golf course. I mean, my gosh, it's so darn beautiful.* He swept a miniature hand across the river valley and the blue outlines of the mountains and desert. *What do you think a place like that sells for?* He pointed to a whitewashed, peak-roofed, refurbished farmhouse on a scrubland slope on the other side of the river. I looked at it over my shoulder. It was a tidy plastered building with a stone foundation and flower gardens planted in tiers elevated above the encroaching sagebrush and cholla cactus. The sky ran into a sandstone ridge in the background—a filament of brilliant orange light radiated through high nacreous clouds. A weathered wooden cross was set in a pile of basalt stones on the highest plane of the ridge.

I couldn't really say, I said flatly. *I stopped looking at real estate prices a few years ago when I topped out the pay scale.* I doubted the man would want to buy a tract HUD house like mine—otherwise I could've gone into great detail on market nuances. He smiled—or his tiny Cupid lips smirked.

What is it you do?

I'm a public school teacher.

I see. Well, we'd be interested in schools around here. Eileen, he nodded at the girl in the back, *is a sophomore.* The girl popped her gum and smiled lasciviously at me. *We might make our primary residence here, but we'd want to get her into a good school of course.*

Of course.

...

I went to see Spagn after school on Monday when the short break ended. He sat at a student desk in the middle of his classroom hunched in total concentration over a stack of binders. His red novelty pen was

crowned with a pink-dyed bit of chicken feather fluff;
a small plastic heart attached to the end of the pen by a
spring flashed a red light every time he touched it to a
page. *Comrade!* I said loudly, and gave a mock salute. He
looked up through his half inch thick lenses and, grinning, returned the salute. He continued the patter.

The revolution is eternal!

What's up, Mister? I asked in the accents of our
students—Spagn had always liked this imitation. He
responded in kind.

Nada, nada. What's up with you, Mister?

I stood over him and tried to replicate my students' snappy hand jive. Spagn watched bemused, snuf-
fling laughter as I wrapped and jiggled and shook his
hand in as complicated and incomprehensible a way as
possible. I sat beside him and looked across the room at
vestigial marks left on the dry erase board. Under a caricature of Spagn as a perversely muscular, big breasted
stud in a speedo, one of his students had written: Jeff
said that Mr. Spagn was 'the shit' (pg. 127) but Linda
replied harshly, saying Mr. Spagn liked to watch 'dumb-
ass' movies (pgs 190 – 198).

What's happening there? I asked, pursing my lips at
the board.

*We're going over how to include quotations and cita-
tions in research papers. I guess you don't teach that curricu-
lum strand to yours?*

No. I'm lucky if I can get them to put a comma on a

page. I don't even worry about whether it's correctly placed or if it's the only thing on the page.

Bah. Commas are the devil's work anyway.

I looked back at the board. Another caption set beside a crude but effective caricature of a seedily smiling pig in a bowler derby and bowtie read: Porkonstrate (v.) To demonstrate how to pork someone (preferrably a young, attractive, and unusually promiscuous female).

Lamely I said, *The word preferably is misspelled in that little witticism there.*

Aren't you the pedantic one.

I never miss an opportunity to teach.

You and Weis both. Isn't that his line? He imitated Weis' low, fast tone, *I never miss an opportunity to teach.*

I've heard him say that before in his ironic monologues and soliloquys. He went down to the border to one of those big bush farms to hunt feral pigs over the break—speaking of porkonstrating. *He said it was his way of putting meat on the table and beating the Bush Depression. I guess he didn't kill anything, but he's got some funny-ass stories about the yahoos and yokels down there.*

I'm sure it was some kind of outing. Set the F-16s out strafing cover fire around the sperm banks when old Weis is on the loose. How was your break?

Good, good, good, good. The break was good.

Did you go anywhere?

I shook my head. *I stayed here. You?*

I took the family south. Lorie's been asking for a vacation. She doesn't seem to realize how much money I make, or, more to it, how much money I don't make. So I thought of going to Mexico in one of my rare diabolical fits of pure genius.

That's right—you have those once every few years, don't you? Weren't you afraid of swine flu?

That was three years ago—but maybe that explains why we had the place to ourselves and everything was so cheap.

How can you cry poverty? You've been at level III a while, haven't you?

I have—I made level III last year. That's how it is when you have a family, buddy. Money disappears. You hemorrhage money you haven't even earned and never will. You know the saying: It takes a village and long, long lines of credit to raise a child.

Before Spagn could remember that I'd been in a relative state of depression for having no family after my divorce three years ago, I asked about the school performance poetry team to change the subject. It was his first year as coach. He had invited me several times to coach with him and in my colossally weary and undecided way I was still considering it.

How's it going with the poetry team, coach?

Great! They're slamming away. Talk about rushes

of genius—and they're not so rare with those kids. Winton DeMilo—I think you met him?

Yessir.

He's the team captain this year. That kid has poems that I think will not only win at the national slam, but will probably shape the psyches of at least seven generations to come.

He's the kid who spends all his allowance cultivating a kind of noir voodoo priest persona—eyeliner and all? He writes those rapid-fire, twelve track, multiple rhyme, polyrhythmic sequence poems about identity politics and the void and the phony messiah and whatnot?

That's him.

I've heard him. He is amazing.

He's a senior this year. You should really come check the team out. That invitation to help coach is always open.

I nodded slowly, reflectively. *It would be interesting to work with kids who are self-motivated and join clubs and actually want to learn the content. I'll mull on it. We have some time before nationals, right?*

Only three months, so let me know. Come as a chaperone at the very least. Don't you have yours writing poetry?

I do, yes.

What interests those kids?

Oh man, you know, all that MTV cocoa boogie reality TV jackass bullshit. They write a lot about guns and rum and blunts and bitches and benzes, etcetera, etcetera. The girls write volumes of ultra-maudlin love poetry—I thought it was forever and ever—*that kind of stuff. They all write some very straightforward fuck-the-world lines, which I've begun to appreciate more and more. Once in a while they surprise me with a word or phrase.*

Sounds civilized enough.

Civilized is as civilized does, buddy. Speaking of which, did you know The Savages are moving to town?

The savages? Are they?

Believe it.

Spagn paused to consider the significance of this fact. *This merit pay bullshit must be their idea then.* There was no irony in how he said it.

You don't like the idea of merit pay?

He scowled. *It'll mean doing nothing but teaching to standardized tests.*

Maybe. Those tests aren't too horrible—some of what's in them is worth learning. I guess we have an advantage in that our students have nowhere to go but up. But when they don't go up enough, we're screwed.

Yeah. I don't know. I just want to be able to teach broader content. Anyway, the union will never allow it. Merit pay means giving up tenure and no one in this dog-eat-ass, political little town will want that.

True, true. No, you're right, the standardized tests are

bullshit. Chalk it up to the progress of man.

I stood up and walked to the dry erase board to read a caption that was only visible as a blur from across the room: Whorable (adj.) Someone or something that is turned into a whore with great ease.

I stared cockeyed at Spagn and reproved in the mechanical, nasally, put on voice of a humpbacked principal or concerned parent.

Is this the content you teach your Language Arts classes, Mister Spagn?

I wish it was. They come up with that all on their own.

I walked back across the room and sat down again giving Spagn a Spaniel look. *You'll be happy,* I said lightly mocking, *to know I saw Tina Hartz in Alphix the other day. She's alive—you didn't ruin her completely, not for lack of trying.* Tina had very briefly been one of Spagn's girlfriends when we were in high school.

Really? he asked in a surprised, serious tone. Spagn was always ingenuous and sincerely interested in everything and everyone—two of the many virtues that made him universally attractive to all but the most bogus of people. *God, man, I haven't seen her since we were walking these halls ourselves two hundred years ago. How did she look?*

She'd looked much, much thinner. Her hair was cropped in overlaid, highlighted hackles and her gaunt face showed she'd internalized an inhuman amount of sorrow, but she was still upright and had traces of the unique style and humor I remembered. I'd asked if she had any children and she said she couldn't afford most men's *stud fees*. She told me her last boyfriend cooked elaborate gourmet meals for ten people, ate a few bites, refrigerated the rest and went into apoplectic screaming fits when she tried to throw out the mildewed remains weeks later. She was in Alphix alone buying herself an Easter lily and two bottles of wine.

She looked as though time hasn't touched her at all, I said.

...

I sat on a thrift store wooden chair in my bedroom on the Sunday of the second break. The back door was open for the first time in months. I could see Highway 518 and a pale green water tower on the hardpan plain leading to the foothills. The mountains were still snowcapped. A wind was whipping tumbleweeds in spirals around telephone poles outside my development block. I called Pops on my cell phone.

What's up, kid? Are you finally defrosting your scrawny ass out there?

It's warmed up, thank Yeshua, but I can't take another winter like that.

You don't sound so good.

Yeah. I don't know what's going on with me, Pops. I don't have much patience lately. I'm exhausted half the time. I paused trying to sum up my complaint. *And The Savages are moving to town—now that the town fathers saw fit to build a golf course.*

The savages have been moving to town since the world began. Do you have a girlfriend yet?

No.

Damn, son, what's it been, three years? You just need to get your dick sticky.

Christ, Pops. Pops was as easily and openly tender as he was vulgar. One of his favorite stories about me was when I was three years old and kept asking—or insisting with perfect recall—that he buy me a *thaw and serve crumble cookie chocolate satin cream cake.* He was both appalled and impressed by my ability to recite that complex litany—though I pronounced *crumble* as *cwumble* and *cream* as *cweam,* as he always pointed out.

Christ nothing. Come down here and get laid for Gasparilla. You have your spring break now, right?

No, that was last week and Easter break ends today. What's Gasparilla?

It's some kind of festival on the beach—one big drunk—college girls flashing their tits for beads. That kind of thing.

Sounds uplifting.

You need to stop obsessing about what's her twat. I

mean it. It's been three years. You need to move on.

It's not her. It's not anything. I'm just tired all the time. And, I thought, *angry and sarcastic and brittle and I keep wishing people's heads would explode.*

A good blowjob will jumpstart you. Pops was relentless.

I would love to meet a good woman, Pops. That's not it at all. I'm ready to meet a woman. I think it will happen when I get my own shit straight.

Luis, nobody ever has their shit straight. Nobody. If there's one piece of wisdom I can pass on to you, it's that. Remember it—you'll hear it said many different ways. No one ever has their shit just so. Maybe that's your problem right there: you're trying too hard to get everything just right and fucking your own head up when it doesn't get there.

I exhaled until I was dizzy.

Maybe, Pops. Maybe.

...

I'd learned from Spagn and Weis and all of the other veteran teachers I'd gone to high school with that it was important to trick my classroom out in a way that would be subconsciously impressive to students. Weis had told me about a study showing reduced behavioral problems in classrooms with plants in them, so I bought

a few hardy species of fern that required minimal care
and placed them in the sills of my two windows. I also
bought a Persian leopard gecko and outfitted an aquarium with Little Homie figurines and Hot Wheels cars
for her. Priscilla Cortez, one of my outspoken students,
called the lizard Honky, because of its pale undersides,
and the name was instantly unanimous. I clipped what
I thought were funny police blotter excerpts and glued
them to a piece of cardboard laid against the back wall
of Honky's habitat:

*Caller reported that there was a strange woman in his car
barking like a dog and laughing.*

*Caller reported that a man accompanied by a dwarf was
harassing a cocktail waitress.*

*Caller reported that he had been run over twice by a Honda
but was all right.*

*Caller reported that a man with a whiskey bottle was block-
ing traffic and screaming obscenities about Jesus.*

*Caller reported that a couple of Chihuahuas and a pit bull
came after her whenever she went outside and she was tired
of it.*

My students appreciated this ecosystem and were eager to help take care of Honky. Several of them rotated the duty of feeding her crickets—a spectacle that enthralled them all even though some of the girls made an obligatory show of being squeamish and terrified.

If nothing else, I reminded myself, despite this zombie funk, I was still a good teacher. A good teacher....

I stood over Honky's aquarium watching her climb a dried ocotillo stick. I had strung mini plastic monkeys along the bottom of it—Honkey ignored them as she stalked a cricket. Carpio Martinez, the Native American student I tutored for morning elective, was late. At 8:12 he walked in so quietly I wouldn't have known he was there if I wasn't facing the door. I looked at the clock on the wall above my desk as he put his hands up and said, *Sorry, sorry, sorry.* I had already given him three or four rounds of the *this-is-it* speech. I decided quickly that I would go through it one last time before calling in his parents and the head teacher.

Carpio....

I know, I know, don't tell me. I couldn't wake up this morning.

He was being somewhat truthful—my students knew too well how this tactic worked with me. I was relieved to be less stern.

What, were you partying on a Wednesday night?

Oh, I party every night. I had to help Brandi. She

was passed out by the side of the road and she lost her shoes.

Brandi was another Native American student at the school—a sullen, dark girl who sounded like she'd inhaled helium on the few occasions when she spoke.

Ok, well, you're a senior. You have six weeks of school left and then you're finally done after twelve years of insti- tutionalization. That's only thirty days of showing up and doing what you have to. Do you get that?

Yeah.

I went on for a few minutes about the country being in the midst of an economic depression, adults making the right choices, the horrors of the world with a high school diploma much less without one, how I'd have to bring in heavier people to resolve the issue if there wasn't a turnaround, etcetera. Carpio stared in- scrutably at the floorboards and mumbled, *yeah*s and *Ok*s. He was one of my favorite students: quiet, respect- ful, careful to avoid the endless shrieking dramas of other students, hardworking and smart when he showed up. He wore nothing but various cutoff T-shirts, para- chute pants and a Washington Redskins cap—which showed a deep—if only partly articulated—humorous sense of power and race politics that I especially ap- preciated. His father worked in the War Chief's of- fice—his large family was as prestigious as it was tragic. One of his uncles had caught his wife cheating, chained her to the back of his truck and dragged her three miles to the tribal police station where he turned himself in. One cousin was a famous artist and actor. We usually spent most of the tutorial talking about the intricacies of life on the reservation—at the end of the hour I'd ask him to write a summary of what we'd discussed. Carpio rubbed his left knuckles with his right hand while I lectured. He had a tattoo of a little balloon—signifying the daughter who'd died an hour after being born—on his neck, and he touched that too: a signal of his impatience.

So that's that, man, I said to cap the authoritarian cautions. *And seriously now, what are you going to do after school? Are you going to do that internship detailing cars that Ms. Starks got you?*

He looked up at me. *I don't know. I was thinking about firefighting too. I think I need to get off the rez for a while.*

That sounds smart. It's always good to travel. Firefighting is hard dangerous work, but I know you'd be good at it. I know the leader of the Hotshots team for this district. I'll talk to him.

Carpio nodded mildly and looked away. *I was also thinking about joining the army.*

What?

He glanced at me, vaguely interested in the vehemence of my response. *Yeah—the army.*

I was openly critical of the government as often and to whatever excess was possible in my class. In the ten-minute public communications exercise I used to open each period, I would rail about carefully chosen issues from the day's headlines while my students watched me with blank faces. Antoinette Apodaca—my only student with a dry sense of humor—drew sketches of me saying *blah blah blah blah* in a cartoon bubble and turned them in as extra credit after my rants. I had spewed at length many times about never being so stupid as to become a cog in the war machine, an instrument of white transnational corporate power, a trigger-bitch for The Man, blah blah blah.

What about all of that talk about Brown Power? Carpio's signature graffitti tag was a sleek futuristic BP with his code name, Carp, under it. He looked contemplative and said nothing. Outside, a blue jay nestled in the crotch of a Chinese Elm and trilled and squawked.

You're really thinking—my voice was perfectly pitched at a cool incredulousness—*about going to Iran to kill other brown people to make a few fat old white men richer?*

I knew you'd say all that stuff. He grinned sheepishly.

As smart as you are, I'm surprised to hear you're even thinking about this. I wondered if it was selfish that I was glad to finally be entirely passionate about something if only for a few minutes.

Don't you want to have a girlfriend, maybe get married?

He sniffed. *Not to none of these crazy-ass chicken heads around here.*

Listen, I said, having a sudden inspiration, *You're just old enough to remember that the war in Iran really started with the war in Iraq. You know that right?*

I guess.

It's a fact. It all happened a few presidents ago, so people forget, but it's a fact. George Bush started the war in Iraq so, even though he was out of office—if he was ever really in office—he started this war too. He and all his fat cat friends.

So?

So I'll make a deal with you: Bush has two daughters a bit older than you but young enough still—here's the deal: if they enlist, because this war is so important to national salvation, then I'll quit teaching and you and I will enlist together. We'll volunteer for the front of the front lines with the Bush daughters. We'll call it the Barbie Brigade.

Carpio whickered like a horse—his laugh. His wide, brutal, indigenous face creased. He gave me a strange, mischievous lemur-eyed look and shrugged. *I don't know, Mister. I'll think about it.*

...

Finally the wind stopped in the late afternoon on Friday. Around three, I read the last of my students' papers. Since every student in the school was in some degree illiterate, I'd had the idea of allowing them to write notes to one another and called the exercise *silent dia-logues* in my planner. Today, Pepito Romero had written a series of violent insights about his ex-girlfriend's new relationship with his ex-best friend, Leon Alvarez—the crassest and most revealing among them being: *evry time that fagget kises her he gonna b tasting my dick in his mouth.* Carmen Lucero, Pepito's writing partner who had repeatedly scrawled *LOL* in shaky capital letters everywhere else in the correspondence, here wrote *ha ha ha ur fucking crazy fool.* Normally I would have gone to make a copy of this uninhibited exchange and shown it to Carl, the math teacher, but I was too unmotivated to do even that. It was a very bad sign. I had been through three years of wreckage, oozing and unspooling, but this was too much. I had to rally myself somehow. I was still a good teacher.

...

I drove to the greenbelt listening to the radio, turning it as far down as possible when the DJ was talk-ing and selling. Music redeemed—but after every song there was an ad for detergent or dog food or tampons: all the engines of modern living. I put an old Sainted Cannibal Apes CD into the player and skipped to their anthem, *Designer Despair.* Drums, bass and a scratchy, minimalistic, agonized guitar riff built frantically out of nowhere. On the off-beat the singer wailed:

Mind gone into supernova/Eating a mocha tort/Too far

*gone by half/To hear God scream abort so/Set out the donuts
Mommy/Increase the viral load/For all those humanoids
and junkies/In survival mode*

Again—weirdly—as I was about to cross the
same bent barbed wire fence on my way to the river,
a couple pulled up to ask directions. Dan and Stella
Slaughter from Amarillo driving in a black Ford Triton
V10 with glittery curving green flames painted on the
hood and sides. They had already bought a four thou-
sand square foot spec house in the Wermer Heights and
they just absolutely loved it to death.

...

I felt the change begin on Wednesday during
my third period prep. Emmie Rodriguez and Michelle
Concha were eating BerryBerry Kix, drinking chocolate
milk and working on their grid drawings in the kitchen.
Al, the head teacher, and Carl strained mightily to get
all of our students involved in what turned out—despite endless resistance—to be extremely sophisticated
compositions in colored pencil. Emmie was blending a
dominatrix's black leather and lace outfit with a neutral
Prismacolor; Michelle outlined the barrel of a gun in
her drawing with a marker. Either they hadn't noticed
I'd come in or didn't care. They talked on without even
glancing at me.

Annastasia's a bitch, man. She fucking thinks she's all that, but she ain't shit.

I know. She's always talking shit. She deserved to get her ass kick at the dance. She was flirting with Viola's boy-friend. Did you see Viola slam her head into that post?

I interrupted.

What are you girls doing down here?

Emmie was a pliable girl who was respectful in one on one situations, but who would talk back snidely if led by her friends. Michelle Concha, a short, moony looking half Mexican, half Native American girl, was brilliant and meticulous with her schoolwork when she wasn't screaming *FUCK* in a blackout rage. The word *fuck* had been branded onto every third neuron in her otherwise beautiful brain. I liked her immensely: she had survived her father dying in a drunk-driving ac-cident, her slobbering rapist uncles, a catatonic mother and nth other holocausts—a final example of resilience. She was the only female student at school who didn't spend every break, lunch period and whatever time snuck in class putting on excessive makeup. The prob-lem was she couldn't be trusted not to start screaming obscenities and she was hostile to any authority. I ex-pected her to give me a hateful stare and start spitting about minding my own fucking business, getting out of her fucking bubble, giving her a fucking break, etcetera. She looked at me now with a cold appraising glance and then amazingly spoke like a student eager to ex-plain circumstances and please her teacher.

Mister Al said we could work down here cuz all those chicken head bitches were talking shit and I almost got into it with Natalie.

Surprisingly—considering how rare it was she was this approachable—I pressed on.

Ok, ok. Well, you can work down here then, but please, please don't call other girls bitches or whatever else and please don't glorify other students getting into fights. It's a form of instigating.

I wondered if Michelle recognized the crushed insect under my insistent professionalism or if she could sense that what was good in me cared about her and wanted to see her empowered. Whatever it was she said, *Ok Mister. Cool.* I smiled wanting to laugh; my head lightened intensely. I said, *Cool.*

As I left the kitchen, to restore her defiant image, she whispered to Emmie, *I need to smoke a big joint of purple haired cush every morning to make it in this place, man.*

. . .

Sitting on a couch in Weis' house while other people mingled, I asked myself if isolation was the cause or a symptom of my depression. I didn't want to be at this party, but here I was, working through it, right? A woman on the other end of the couch was telling a man seated elbows to knees in a blue lounge chair that she only finally decided to divorce her husband after he'd denied her sex for six years and her hair started falling out. I thought of Darla, the secretary at school telling me in her scatty way—after a long discourse on how she had to take zinc pills every morning or her hands shook—that after what sounded like a completely heinous decade of marriage, she'd stayed with her husband for another year while he finished plastering their house. As soon as he'd troweled on the last scoop, she served him the papers.

What, I thought of my ex-wife, *did she endure before she decided to leave me?* I watched the man reach for a wheat cracker smeared with brie as he said, *Wow*, to the woman's frank revelation. She went on talking about her ex-husband's second wife, a *waifish froofroo girly girl nonentity* who'd just had a disc nucleoplasty done. *Wow*, the man said again, reaching for another cracker. *Nothing*, I answered myself, *I did nothing to her but show love and appreciation while she was out sampling dick*, and I felt like the napalm jelly that had been coating my nerve endings for three years began to dissolve. I felt the beginning tickles and scratches of an all-seizing laughter that frightened me.

And Weis, in fact, commented on how giddy and giggly I suddenly was. Drinking a tall Slurry (two ounces Cana, one ounce vodka mixed with tonic and lime juice), lean and pop-eyed with satanic eyebrows, Weis sat beside me and gave an atomically detailed, manic, stream of consciousness account of his hunting trip near the border—boiling days of futile squirming around through thorny brush culminating in a party at a massive deluxe ranch house owned by some Hollywood megaslick public relations maven who flew there in his Cessna twice a year to get out of the city. The yokels loved him and the season ending fete at his place was the gala event of the year. Weis looked fevered and spun out, as usual, in the rapid fire telling:

A hundred goddamn miles of totally insane thorn scrub in every direction and this guy has a bathtub full of ice, high end, $500 per bottle French champagne and fresh oysters. There're the heads of fifty or more feral hogs on the walls and all the local hicks—a bunch of guys in Stetsons and ostrich skin boots, chawing tobacco and their hound dog Gideon baying out in the yard—these guys are all having some kind of pissing contest with their belt buckles—can you imagine? Belt buckles are all the rage down there—the smallest one must have weighed fifty pounds. Big crazy deals: steer heads and feral hogs made out of abalone, garnets, turquoise and Mexican silver and whatnot—the best was one of those riverboat gambler's guns with a pearl handle....

Weis showed all of his pointy pearlescent teeth to emphasize the humor and craziness of the scene. (Although one large front tooth and one canine were yellowish). I giggled and continued to giggle when Weis began talking about a mutual friend who had just come back from a trip to Thailand where he'd seen a woman smoke cigarettes and throw darts with her vagina—which was only impressive because she smoked unfiltereds and was so accurate with her shots, hitting one bullseye after another after another.

The reason, Weis raved on, *Petie said it was weird as hell over there though, of all things, of all fucking things, ha, ha, was that the Thais are supposed to be all-accepting super-Buddha types right, but he, ha, ha, ha, just like Petie, classic Petie—he got the vibe, ha, ha,* the vibe, *right, that they, the Thai men, resented the hell out of him because he was quote unquote* big dicking *their women. That was his term,* big dicking—*you know, like stretching them out so that they wouldn't ever be able to marry a local guy because they wouldn't be able to feel his cock unless they got their hymens surgically reconstructed, which I guess half of them actually do, it's a big surgical craze and half the women do it just to do it, the half that aren't ladyboys which is the name they give to the men who have sex changes and who are all so petite you can't even tell the difference between them and real women until the dress comes off according to Petie....*

Weis' stopped talking when his beautiful, squealing, three-year-old daughter, Helena, ran over and writhed onto his lap saying, *Hold me, daddy*, but I kept giggling. I giggled and held my flushed face in my hands until the end of the night when Weis told me at the door in a scathing deadpan that I was totally hysterical, had been hysterical the whole night—then I laughed.

...

I was still laughing on the Friday when school

ended for the year and I had driven to the greenbelt and made it several steps past the bent barbed wire fence toward the river when Zeke and Mildred Butcher and their triplet sons, Buford, Billy and Bart honked at me in their Chrysler Pacifica. For a long second—in an attempt to contain myself before I turned to walk back to the road and give them directions—I looked west toward the river where every tree and all of the ground was in full blossom—radiant waves and puffs of brightest pigment everywhere. But I couldn't stop snorting and laughing.

I was still laughing when Carpio sent me a postcard from Camp Doha—the picture was of a Muslim woman in full burkah firing a machine gun, and on the back in his circumspect script he'd written: *Yo Mister. The Barbie Brigade.* I was still ha, ha, ha laughing, almost choking when I saw Carpio in town a year later. His eyes were incurious and moved slowly over the storefronts. He told me dully, unhurriedly, that he was reenlisting. I laughed—a queer gurgling sound—at his punch line: *Beats working at Wal-Mart, Mister.*

Just One Dollar

I hadn't seen Earl in the six months since his daughter's fifth birthday—a memorable June Tuesday because the day before, the mayor had sent one of his lieutenants on some errand in his new burgundy Cadillac Brougham and the flunky had swerved to avoid a stray cat and flipped the car four times down Bay Drive into the stucco wall of the Moss Feaster Funeral Home. Earl and I sat in the living room laughing uncontrollably at the headline. Miraculously no one had been hurt, and while the mayor—who was a thoroughbred, red faced asshole with a pro-condominium agenda—was undoubtedly doubly insured for his losses, he must've been sputtering some prickly expletives from behind the big desk in his oak paneled office.

Earl's daughter came into the tiny living room of his efficiency apartment as we wept over a photo of the demolished car in the newspaper. She gave us cake on paper plates, primly pointing out that she'd made sure we each had flowers on our pieces. Earl looked at the chocolate icing rosettes Charlotte had insisted her grandmother cut out for us, and I sensed he knew his purpose now and wouldn't disappear again. But—to quote Earl himself—*it all gets lost between the cola and the chrome*: that afternoon, after Charlotte's friends had left, he was back in the streets hustling Christ only knows what for oxycontins.

I'd met Earl at the midnight Narcotics Anonymous meeting at Saint Catherine's on Bellaire Avenue two years earlier, just after I moved. I was at the meeting with my father—an NA veteran of twenty-two years. I've only ever had the occasional drink or joint because of the endless stories of insane vomiting ruin I'd heard going to those meetings with Pops every summer vacation since I was nine. One cautionary tale in particular, told by an obese, puffing woman with a thin frizzled roach of white blonde hair—an unemotional exhausted account of waking up with her pants at her ankles on a street corner for the millionth time—had left a permanent impression. Now that I lived in the area, I still went to three meetings a week to get my *half assed recovery*, to use Pop's phrase.

That night two years ago Earl—at his first meeting—sat next to Pops and me staring noncommittally out a window of the Youth Recreation Building at flocks of wild parakeets moving through the crepe myrtle trees on the church cemetery grounds while a plump pimply teenager wearing a John Deere cap shared that he was a *grimy motherfucking addict* who would steal anything and everything from you to get high, then pat you on the back and cry openly with you in consolation while cursing the motherfucking thief the next day. When the meeting closed with the usual group invocations, Earl said *just to get laid* instead of *just for today* just loudly enough for me to hear. We laughed, hugged and introduced ourselves. Everyone went to the nearby Outback Restaurant afterward and Earl, Pops and I sat together at a table revising the serenity prayer to fit modern conditions. We had a ready version by the time the Bloomin' Onions and steaks arrived. Earl read it off a napkin to the waitress:

God, grant us the senility to accept the things we cannot change

The guns and hard cash to change the things we can

And the Ouija Board to know the difference

    The waitress—nearing middle age, falsely brunette, wearing acrylic press-on nails and the Outback staff uniform—didn't need any come-ons. Lisa or Leslie—she was with Earl a week before he was back out using drugs with her.

...

I went twice to Earl's apartment in the half year he'd been gone. The second time there I met Mr. Delmont, the landlord, on the stairs. He was wearing a pale blue polo shirt and a yellow ascot and kept fussily smoothing his pencil mustache with his pinkie. His cologne was stronger than the rank salt smell of the inter-coastal marsh behind the apartment block. Earl had called him a *morose, carp-lipped old fag who had to pay callboys the premium for the stink finger* and I'd recognized the intense furtive hunger in his rheumy gibbous stare ever since.

Hello Luis. Mr. Delmont's mealy passive-aggressive voice grated. I sensed he wanted to be an openly flamboyant lisping homosexual but was incapable of it for programming reasons. *Any word from Earl, Luis?* Repeating your name constantly was his one trick of speech.

No, Mr. Delmont. Nothing yet. I have a few ideas about where to look though.

He smiled. His teeth were large, horsey, nicotine stained.

Well, that's good. That's something at least. You'll let me know, Luis?

During my first visit, I'd spoken with Mr. Delmont at exhausting length about the practical details of Charlotte and her grandmother, Kathleen, staying in the apartment after Earl disappeared. He had complained about the legal technicalities and complications of having tenants in one of his efficiencies who had not signed the lease. He had gone on and on about obscure housing statutes so as to have an excuse—I was sure—for staring ravenously at me. I didn't know if he was making the crap up as he went. *Section nine, article three is explicitly clear, Luis….* It was a drably impressive display either way. He was, in fact, being generous to allow Kathleen and Charlotte to stay. He had the excuse of someone owed something for his walleyed staring now.

I will definitely let you know. I looked beyond him up the stairwell.

That'll be fine, he muttered as I passed. *That'll be fine, Luis.*

...

Earl's apartment was on the third floor of the five story Sea View Apartments block. Out the living room window, to the left, I could see the bristling foliage of black mangroves covering both sides of the inter-coastal channel, but the ocean was invisible somewhere behind a serried skyline of pale pastel colored condominiums on the strip. The clearest view from the window was of the humungous red neon crab on the shingle roof of Barnacle Bill's Crab Shack. I stood looking at the Crab Shack parking lot waiting for Kathleen to bring me a cup of coffee. A white egret stalked across the pavement into a spotty dun-colored lot of sand and sea oats behind an unpainted cinderblock pawn shop. Two black men with a bucket between them sat fishing from the calcimined pedestrian bridge over the inter-coastal channel. Charlotte came into the living room holding a Malibu Barbie doll at her chest.

Hi, Luis. Her voice was small and serious. She had Earl's large, aloof, dark eyes.

Hi, babygirl. What's up?

My daddy's not here right now, she said importantly.

I know. I know. He'll be back.

When?

I'm sorry I don't know that.

Oh.

But I'm looking for him and I know he's thinking of you. He's just working out a few things right now. I hope you know he really loves you.

I know that, she said as though I had stated something all too obvious.

Good. It's good you know that.

She dropped her Barbie and ran to the couch. *Look, I made a picture for daddy.*

With a serious face, she brought me the drawing done on a rough blue piece of construction paper: two stick figures—her father and her —holding hands under a palm tree beside a box house with windows and curtains.

It's beautiful! But where's the sun? You should draw the sun above the house there.

Ok! She laughed excitedly and ran back to the couch to get her crayons. I watched her draw a circle and radial lines around it: the sun, glowering star, giver of life.

...

Five years ago, Earl had been a heroin addict who, after several attempts, had detoxed and stayed clean by going to NA meetings every night. Pops was his sponsor—a stern and natural mentor for radical life changes. He'd gotten Earl a maintenance job at the municipal hospital and loaned him the money to buy a '71 Chevette through an inside connection at a police auction. The car was a mint condition classic after he had it reupholstered to cover the .22 bullet holes in the back seat. He met Angelique in the rooms when he was one year and three months clean. She gave birth to Charlotte a year later and looked terrified, withdrawn and skeletal for the five months afterward before she went back to stripping and using heroin. Two weeks later she was remarried to a 65-year-old real estate developer and lived in an 8,000 square foot mansion on Crescent Estates Drive. Earl stayed clean even though he was devastated—more than anything for Charlotte, who would grow up motherless. Kathleen, his stepmother, a stolid, heavyset, grunting Midwestern woman with an overbite moved from Kansas with Romeo and Goliath, her pugs, into the bedroom of Earl's efficiency. She slept there with Charlotte; Earl slept on a fold out couch in the living room.

They survived—they managed. Earl rationalized Angelique's departure with the durable phrase: *I'd never work a day in my life either if I had a pretty face and a pussy*. We got together almost every day after work at the Denny's off of Highway 17. I liked his uninvolved otherworldly manner and submerged air of hilarity. He would stare out the window at the flower beds in the highway median talking comically about the routines of his workday, then glance at me with familiar irony to deliver a punch line. I think I've always needed an older brother—something—and Earl was it.

Then he broke his wrist when a wrench slipped while he was fixing a pipe in the hospital basement. He went to a pain clinic and was prescribed fifteen milligrams of oxycontin four times a day for the pain. He went back when the script ran out, paid the doctor the $100 consultation fee and was moved up to thirty milligrams six times a day. Within the month he was shooting eighty milligrams eight times a day and had been coming and going since.

...

Kathleen had heard nothing at all from or about Earl. She looked at me with watery eyes until I said that I'd thought to go to the men's shelter and ask around. He'd stayed there for short periods before while out using, and I vaguely knew the first shift director, Randolph Myers, because he had dated my colleague, Ms. Clapp, the 8th Grade Home Economics teacher at Pierson High.

I had to take the beach trolley downtown and sat waiting over an hour for it at the Hilton stop. I watched the ocean hissing past the tennis courts and a manicured grove of royal palms. The public beach was set apart by a rubble wall of bleached coral and a spiky sedge of wild palmetto. Shrieking gulls dove at open dumpsters in the service alley. The air smelled of fried food and the sea. A woman in a pink Pima cotton business suit and Bvulgari sunglasses came out of the Hilton entrance speaking rapidly into her Bluetooth. Her heels rung sharply on the road as she passed me on her way to a silver Mercedes. She snorted and looked furiously at the ground.

Freddie, you know how many peoples' asses I had to bloody to restructure that department and I'm not going to let Carlyle or any of his associates steamroll me and undo what I've done no matter how close he is to Danson's or Burke's people. Listen, I tried to tell Wilcox—I tried to tell him. I said to him, I said, Look, Steve, you've got a BU policy and a solid opt out policy that contradicts everything in it. *I know. I know that, Freddie. I told him there was no goddamn way Kawalski was going to get any PM time at all. Ten minutes later, Stan Edgars calls me—he was the one who was leaving last year right when we were bidding on a transcom with the navy—anyway, he calls me less than ten minutes after I'm off the phone with Wilcox and says there's nothing he can do because Hazen is giving him directives and meanwhile Rosenbaum's on vacation with strict orders not to call or text, not to email, nothing— he's totally incommunicado and I realized Wilcox is probably lameducked by the Board and he can't—bingo! Exactly, Freddie! Exactly! Arnold and everyone else know that he's got no lash up with Fisk so he can't prop any of the newer bids or products and all along there was that problem from the start because the JV2 contractor supposedly hates Weinstein—no one knows why—so that's a horrible source selection bias from the word go and everyone in that department isn't perceived to be aggressive enough in the new environment as it is, so the long and the short of it is that Dick is in the headlights now—yup. Yup. Exactly. He thinks he could be fired any day and if that happens you can be sure I'll have some strong words with Carlyle, damn it!*

She climbed into the Mercedes and sped away soundlessly. Curlews perched on a telephone wire clicking and cheeping. A slight, stringy juvenile with a spiked green Mohawk, wearing fake snakeskin pants and a muscle shirt with a faded snarling image of the Madonna screaming into a microphone on it sat next to me murmuring into his Blackberry: *Get this bro: we should make, like, instead of like gummy bears we could make gummy fetuses and sell them to the tourists, ha ha!*

...

Two derelicts stinking of alcohol sat in front of me on the trolley. One—a dwarfish sunburned man with no front teeth—spoke and sprayed while the other—tall, stooped, lugubrious—looked at his knees nodding and swallowing. *First thing I done when I got in common cell was walk right up to a big buck nigger named Bambi and punch 'im for all I was worth. Bam, man! Right in 'is face! You gotta do that when you in, man, other'ise you gonna be Bubba's bitch, sure as shit.*

We passed rows of beach cottages until we came over the bridge—the highway widened into a three-lane fronted by used car dealerships, pawn shops, liquor and drug stores, trailers and small churches. A wide, igneous red band of light arced above the several thirty-plus story financial buildings across the bay.

I got off the trolley behind the two bums in front of the men's shelter—a weathered brick building with a small fenced in backyard and two portable sleeping quarters. A single saw palm grew near the sidewalk leading to the entrance. The many finches dotting it swept away in a loud flutter as I followed the men into the building.

In the entry foyer, a freckled, roly-poly woman in a polka dot dress, watched me with bovine curiosity. *I'm looking for Randolph Myers.* She swept her hands across her red bobbed bangs and looked at a small slip of paper. *Are you Luis Markel?* I nodded yes. She spoke into a phone in a high pitch Bronx accent—a surprising and unnerving voice, though I could hardly hear her behind the partition glass.

He isn't inside yet; he's in the sleepers but he says to go in an' wait. He'll be in in twenny minutes, honey.

I walked down a linoleum tiled hallway hung with crude watercolors of sailboats and came into the recreation area. More than a hundred surrealistically scrofulous men sat in donated chairs and couches in a high ceilinged whitewashed hall that smelled of Lysol, urine and cabbage. Most of them were in a semicircle watching *Wheel of Fortune* on a big screen TV. Another subgroup of men set at round foldout tables playing checkers. I sat on a couch without springs next to a withered black man in dirty faded digital camo fatigues and a cut off shirt with a half effaced picture of Loni Anderson on it. His gray dreadlocks became one massive tangle on his back. He had an unhinged, bulging, leery look.

You ain't homeless, man.

No.

Wachoo doin' down here then?

I came looking for a friend. Earl Watts. You know him?

The question seemed to make him feel easier about me.

Earl Watts. Earl Watts. Big huge black dude?

No. My size. White.

No, man, I don't know 'im.

He might not even have come around.

Wachoo do? The man asked abruptly.

Me? I'm a teacher.

A teacher, huh?

I teach Language Arts and Humanities at Pierson Middle School.

Yeah? You like it?

I do. I used to teach troubled kids, and they were great for different reasons, but now I'm teaching kids who are very eager to learn and curious.

Troubled how?

Kids with learning and behavioral disabilities. Kids from broken home environments.

Whats'a difference? They all troubled nowadays.

Well, the kids I teach now are happy to…uh…to be in school. They want to learn. They're interested in what I have to say. One girl just wrote an essay for me about how her cousin has four nipples because when he was in the womb he had a twin who wasn't born.

Oh yeah? No shit? His eyes widened then slitted; his nostrils flared.

Yeah. Another one wrote a short story about a man who supports himself and his family by winning eating contests. That kind of thing. Very imaginative.

Alright, alright. I getchoo, young blood. Now I'm gonna tell you somethin'.

OK.

My parents was communists, OK, back in the civil rights times, you know what I'm sayin'.

Yeah.

My name, Karl. You feel me?

Yes.

Now, I come up, hard, man, you know what I'm sayin'. I ain't one these platinum blond niggaz drivin' a Jaguar XKR like they do, man. I come up on collard green in the projects, you know what I'm sayin'? My folks, they taught me all that communist thinkin' right: to each according to his need, from each according to his ability *and all that, but I tell you somethin' straight out right now: I* wants *me some bling bling, man; I wanna get me a little bijou bijou, boy, you know what I'm sayin'.*

Sure. I can understand that.

See right there, right there. Check that shit out. He pointed to the TV. Pat Sajack was prompting a dowdy, big shouldered woman in a pink dress to spin the wheel and solve the puzzle. Only three letters were revealed. The clue was: A seaside meal. Karl said, *Right there, man, right there. The answer is mahi mahi with lemon, man. These contestants don't know shit. You gotta know that Merv Griffin produce this show. You gotta get inside the country club with him; get inside Merv's head, you know what I'm, sayin'.*

I looked incredulously at Vanna White turning over three m's on the board. Karl was right.

That's amazing. You should go on the show.

Yeah, man. Make me some retirement dollars, you know what I'm sayin'. Big money, man. He shook his head as though he could see the stacked piles of hundred dollar bills. *Dinner time now. You want some fish fingers, man?*

No thanks. I've already eaten.

You got any spare change, man?

I gave him a dollar. He looked at it disapprovingly then shambled off toward a double doorway at the other end of the hall. Another man—young, thick and muscular, but with a swollen beer belly, a foreshortened forehead and a shriveled left hand—approached immediately and sat next to me.

Hey, you ever heard of a plexiotomy?

No, I can't say I have.

Well, it's when your head's shoved so far up your ass, they've got to replace your abdomen with plexiglass so that you can see out of it.

He smiled expectantly. I made a quick laughing sound.

I'm working on getting a plexiotomy.com domain

name. Can you see it? I'll sell hats, T shirts, mugs, the whole thing. I was a business major. You gotta buck, bro?.

...

So Luis, if I may ask, how's Melinda?

I sat across Randolph Myer's paper strewn desk looking at a photograph of his daughter—who he'd once told me was in college studying accounting—doing the splits on a football field, her pompoms above her head, her arms and legs naked. Myers was bald, beetling and often unbelievably cheerful. He'd worn a bowtie whenever he came to the school to pick up Ms. Clapp.

Oh, she's alright, I guess. I usually only see her in passing in the halls. No catastrophes that show.

Wonderful. She's a wonderful woman. I'm glad to hear she's doing well, he said hurriedly. *So, what brings you to the bughouse?*

I'm looking for Earl Watts, that old friend of mine who was here a year ago. I wondered if he was back.

Oh no, Randolph's round amiable face puckered with genuine concern. *Is he out using drugs again?*

I'm afraid so.

Hmph. Well, he hasn't been by here, but if he does come through, I'll be sure to call you.

I appreciate that very, very much. I'll say hi to Melinda for you.

He looked intently at the papers on his desk. *Thank you.* He tried a nonchalant laugh—it sounded like he was coughing. *Tell her my number hasn't changed.*

...

As a joke, one of my students had programmed the Death of Disco ringtone into my cell phone and I hadn't changed it. Its quick synthesized bass sounds woke me up at 2:17 a.m. I was tired, having marked papers for hours after dinner, but I came awake immediately thinking someone was dead.

Hello?

Silence.

Hello?

Luis....

Earl?

He wanted to sound jovial but was too stoned.

Hey buddy, it's me.

Earl, where the fuck are you?

Nowhere, man. Nobody's anywhere.

Earl, where are you?

Luis, you remember in…how back in June, 2006 all those bookies from Vegas were taking bets that on the 6th… on June 6th, 2006, the 6th day of the 6th month of the 6th year the world would end because it was, like, 666? You remember that? His voice was manic and thinly tired at the same time.

I do. I remember, but….

You remember that? You remember they were taking bets at over a million to one that the world would end, man, doomsday!

Yes, Earl, but….

…And we were jiving around, man, saying we should take that bet because the payoff was so good….

I'd seen Earl at the end of a sluggish high off a two month oxycontin binge once when I was picking him up—literally—on Dunn's Pier. All of the great knots of desire, alienation and fear had dissolved in him for the moment. Pelicans and petrels flew in close spirals around us as though he was already carrion. His eyes were opaque. He would come down, shaking, moaning and spewing bile everywhere in an hour, but he was untouchable, totally nerveless until then. He must have been in that state now—the last full, invulnerable minutes of a high before the sickness and erasure and biting bugs in the brain.

Earl, man, come on, come on.

You remember? We were going to take that bet at a million to one, man! One dollar gets you a million, man!

Just one dollar!

He was speaking rapidly, ecstatically, but in a scratchy, worn voice.

Earl, what about Charlotte?

Charlotte, Charlotte, Charlotte…. Remember man we were going to take that bet and I'll tell you why it's good we didn't Luis, good we didn't take that bet for even a shitty little fucking dollar.

Earl, Earl, I'll come pick you up. Where are you?

He'd walked in circles around a pillar in a circular room at the rehab center for an entire day, sweating and screaming the last time he'd detoxed.

Listen Luis, listen, it was a hustle, man, a fucking hustle.

I know Earl. I know. Where are you?

It was a hustle, man, because, say we had taken that bet. He was shouting, hysterical. *Say we'd taken that bullshit bet at a million to one and we'd won—we'd won one million dollars and the world ended. What then, motherfucker? How're you going to collect your million dollars if the world's ended? Huh! How motherfucker? It's a fix! You can't win.* He was screaming.

Earl, I know, I know. Listen…Earl.

Silence.

His voice was oddly calm when he spoke again. *Luis, you remember that last shithole I cleaned up in, that city outpatient clinic?*

Yeah, man. Of course.

I was the youngest guy there. They were all sixty, seventy, even eighty years old. The fucking doctors prescribe them oxies for their pain and the next thing they know they're going up the walls withdrawing, feeling their goddamn bones melting! Do you know how much it hurts? DO YOU? DO YOU KNOW HOW MUCH IT HURTS? Those fucking doctors at the pain clinics charge $100 a pop to the fifty people who go through there a day, plus they get a $100 kickback from the pharmaceutical companies for every $250 chit they write. They don't even look at your MRI, man. It's a fix.

I know. I know that Earl, but….

You can't win, Luis.

I know Earl, but you have other things to think about. Other things than winning. You're already a winner. Think of Charlotte. You can do it, man. You know how to do it. You've done it before. Stay steady. I'll come get you. Come on, man! We'll think of what to do next and get you clean.

Silence. I held the phone and stared at a whorl of paint on the bare wall.

Earl?

Nothing.

EARL?

Bang!

www.ingramcontent.com/pod-product-compliance
Lightning Source LLC
Chambersburg PA
CBHW060236180626
46813CB00007B/3109